The "MIRACLE ROSES" - A True Story
A Conduit to St. Therese
Author: Lynda Peringian, MS, RD
FOURTH EDITION

Historical & Amazing Good News - First Book of it Kind - Unique!
Readers Getting Their Wish & Finding Roses! This Book Can Help You!

1. "<u>God</u>" (our Glory goes to Him). **God is at the top** (see front cover).
2. **<u>Under</u> God are "<u>Saints</u>,"** (God's helpers). **"St. Therese"** (one of the saints), **is popular with all <u>religions</u>** (Moslems, Jewish, Christians, etc.). **She is noted as the greatest saint of modern times, and is known for working miracles and roses. Her roses continue to fall everywhere. People seek her healing and guidance.**
3. **Under St. Therese is "<u>Author-Peringian</u>"** (one of St. Therese's helpers). **Peringian's roses** (delivered by a florist) <u>lasted</u> **ten weeks - an historical record! Unbelievable Newspaper Report** (see page 8). **These "<u>MIRACLE ROSES</u>" are providing a <u>Spiritual Connection</u>.**
4. **This book is a "<u>conduit</u>" - helps people connect to God & St. Therese. Author's Advice - <u>Four Steps</u> - How You Can Get Your Prayer Answered** (see page 5). **Readers of this book are reporting blessings, miracles, and finding roses!** (see pages 6 & 7).

ACKNOWLEDGMENT

Thank you everyone who helped especially my gracious mother, Clara Kumjian Peringian, who did edit work. A special thanks to Dennis & Judy Dietrich for being connected to St. Therese, our family, and more. Appreciation goes to Xlibris, librarians, florists & gardeners, who handle roses, & others too numerous to list. To all of you who have not been mentioned here, please know that you have not gone unacknowledged. You will always be remembered forever and in my heart with loving thoughts. THANKS ... all of you!   Lynda Ann Peringian

*Inspiration   *Miracles   *Religion   *Roses   *St. Therese

Peringian, Lynda - Fourth Edition
The "MIRACLE ROSES" – A True Story
A Conduit to St. Therese

Subjects: Inspiration, Miracles, Roses, Religion, St. Therese
Softcover Color Picture Book, 36 pages, Photos

INSPIRATION & REFERENCE BOOK

Copyright © 2004, 2005, 2007, 2010, 2014
by Lynda Peringian, MS, RD

This book is not a substitute for your Koran, Bible, or any other prayer book.

Library of Congress Number: 2004099651

Print information available on the last page

Xlibris

Fourth Edition

ISBN: Softcover   978-1-4771-1871-9
ISBN: EBook   978-1-6641-3840-7

PUBLISHER: XLIBRIS CORPORATION
1663 Liberty Drive #200
Bloomington, Indiana 47403

HOW YOU CAN ORDER THIS BOOK: Ask for Softcover (Color Picture Book) price less than hardback
1. Orders@Xlibris.com   844-714-8691   *We welcome hearing from you!*
Discounts – resellers, garden, florist, nature, prayer & religious groups   1-812-519-5121 ext. 5022
2. www.amazon.com Amazon delivers quick   Free delivery with 2 or more books
3. www.barnesandnoble.com
4. www.shrinechurch.com (see gift shop), (248) 541-4122 ext 418   Mr. Jack Hoolehan

DEDICATION to "St. Therese"

This book is dedicated to St. Therese, who is our most popular saint today worldwide.

St. Therese of Lisieux was born January 2, 1873 in France. Her parents were very loving and her mother died when St. Therese was only four years old. She had four older sisters and her father taught her about helping those who were poor. Unfortunately at nine years old she fell ill from tuberculosis. At the age of fifteen, she entered the convent, which is considered young.

The name of St. Therese of the Child Jesus was given to her because she felt God had called her to serve Him with childhood simplicity. She compared the Saints to flowers & thought of herself as a little flower that would praise God in her everyday actions. She is known as the "Little Flower" and thought of herself as being a small flower in a garden. Therese is known for roses and also as the "Saint of the Little Ways," meaning she believed in doing little things in life well and making others love God. She prayed for others who were less fortunate and dedicated herself to spiritual help through sickness and darkness. She never felt sorry for herself with her illness and had great suffering with her illness.

St. Therese had a great love for missionaries, kept in touch with them often, and later was declared Universal Patroness of the Missions. She kept notes of her remembrances and said, "How unhappy I shall be in heaven if I cannot do little favors on earth." By serving the mission she did a lot of good for people. Her autobiography, "The Story of a Soul," the world came to know her and she is noted to be the "greatest saint in modern times." This book has been translated into 60 languages. She earned her sainthood not only for her great deeds but for her great love. Her "little ways" inspires millions of people worldwide. She passed away at the young age of 24 on September 30, 1897.

"I will spend my heaven in doing good work by helping God work miracles," St. Therese said. She also said, "I will let fall a shower of roses!" She is still active working miracles today by helping God work miracles with people of all faith. People pray for her intercession and ask for a rose to appear, a sign that their prayers may be answered. If you find a rose, perhaps she sent it. Her roses continue to fall everywhere. Readers of this book are reporting blessings, miracles, and other good news. Some are finding roses in unusual places!

CONTENTS

GOALS

This book is an INSPIRATIONAL BOOK and a REFERENCE BOOK for garden, florist, nature, prayer, and religious groups.

The GOALS of this book are:

1. Report the fascinating story of the author's long lasting roses (ten weeks), *"MIRACLE ROSES,"* an historical record. The sequence of events from the delivery day to the rose's last day is explained in detail.
2. Help people understand that God (our glory goes to Him) has helpers called "saints." St. Therese is one of those saints, who is known for roses and working miracles.
3. Help people connect to God and St. Therese with their prayer request. See AUTHOR'S ADVICE - Four (4) Steps How You Can Get Your Prayer Answered - SPIRITUAL CONNECTION (see page 5). This book is a REFERENCE BOOK and is a "conduit" (connector) to God and St. Therese.
4. Help give readers inspiration, hope, and faith. This book is an INSPIRATIONAL BOOK.
5. Review how the author's intercession from God and St. Therese happened with her roses.
6. Discuss St. Therese, our most popular saint worldwide, known with all religions.
7. Discuss the Bible in reference to miracles.
8. Motivate readers to keep their eyes open.
9. Discuss prayers and relaxation.
10. Provide information about roses.
11. Report good news from readers of this book. See Praises & Reader's Reports (pages 6 & 7).
12. Display photos of the Preserved *"MIRACLES ROSES."*

This book has interest for the following SUBJECT headings:

*Inspiration	*Miracles	*Religion	*Roses	*St. Therese

PRAISES & READER'S REPORTS - Reports are coming in everyday

Readers: To submit a Praise, call Xlibris 1-888-795-4275 or mail it to: Lynda Peringian Xlibris Corporation, 1663 Liberty Dr. #200, Bloomington, IN. 47403

"Amazing! My grandson did not need major surgery. My prayer request got answered while reading The "MIRACLE ROSES." Instead a small procedure was done."
Rose Leflere - Almont, MI.

"Everyday this book helps millions of people with it's inspiration & spirituality!"
Bob Patton, MS, PT

"I slept so sound without my medication after reading the book, The "MIRACLE ROSES"- A True Story! This incredible book has inspired me."
Jenny Poole - Oxford, MS

"I think it is the love and dedication in Lynda's heart that made those amazing roses last so long. This world is fortunate to have her in it."
Dr. Eric. L. Matteson - *Mayo Clinic*, Rochester, MN

"The day my sister found out about this book, she was shocked! She saw a live red long stem rose in the middle of the road! She thanked God."
Connie Simmons- Davidson, MI

"This uplifting book inspires readers with her interesting story and messages of hope and faith flow from the pages."
The County Press (Lapeer, MI. newspaper)

"How fortunate to have met the author Peringian! Her book is very inspirational, touched my heart. I am buying copies to give to others so they can also get inspired!"
Nancy L. Peck - IN.

"After just talking about Peringian's book, I saw a beautiful white fresh-cut long stem rose! It was in the middle of my parking lot space at the Costco Store."
Marjorie Yedlin - Michigan

"Wow...after getting my wish, I saw a live white rose on the busy highway!"
Hope Landry - MI.

"After I read Peringian's book, I felt more peace with myself."
Wally Balduck- Michigan

"Wow!...fun and easy to read. Not only is this book extremely helpful to lift your spirits, but everyone will benefit in our tough economic times now."
Joan Cox- Sarasota, Florida

"This true story is a CLASSIC...very unique! God created those miraculous roses and had Peringian write this fascinating story."
Dewey Little (Editor & Writer) - Michigan

"Through a miracle this book gave me comfort and inspiration!"
Judy Arteaga - Normal, Illinois

"Due to recently meeting the author Peringian, I have had many blessings. My one friend's baby, who was very ill, suddenly is getting better!"
Sherry Belka Smith - Michigan

"I believe in the "MIRACLE ROSES!" Within a few weeks I was able to lease our home to a wonderful man."
Katie Goodwin, OTR - Arizona

"A spiritual connection happened recently due to Peringian's book. I had a good change in my life! Not only that, but I noticed a single red rose on the floor."
Judi Pelli - Michigan

"Praise to Lynda, the author, for sharing her "MIRACLE ROSES," and the many blessings and intercessions that are happening to readers of this story. This is very good news for all of us - unbelievable! FIRST BOOK of its kind!"
Fran Nicol (Healthcare Manager) - Michigan

"I was able to get my wish I prayed on, due to the book, The "MIRACLE ROSES" - A True Story. I keep it handy so I can get to it easily."
Matt Kettler (Paramedic)- Michigan

"The book, The "MIRACLE ROSES"- A True Story, is a true miracle!"
Dr. Steve Schweinsberg - TN.

"Amazing! St. Therese connected with Lynda perfectly. Now this book helps answer your prayer request!"
Marilyn Lyman (Editon & Author)- Michigan

"After being inspired by reading Peringian's book, I had a pleasant rose event happen! That evening a beautiful live red rose was next to me and there were no other roses in the restaurant. So many good things happened to me since!"
Mary Ann Gibson - Florida

"A heart warming story with a message about believing!"
Nyal Bischoff (LTC Specialist) - MI.

"This inspirational book is great for classroom study."
Marilyn Wagner (Teacher)- Michigan

"What an inspirational and remarkable story, which is presented well."
William Roush (Attorney)

INTRODUCTION

The story begins in 1999, when my fresh cut roses (delivered by a florist) stayed alive for ten weeks, an historical record! This INCREDIBLE FIND was documented on the front page of the newspaper (see page 8) and witnessed by many people. This book reports the details of my miraculous roses, an intercession (medium) from God and St. Therese (see St. Therese - My Heavenly Friend" pages 20-21). This divine (heaven) intervention (go between) happened the same year, 1999, when St. Therese relics were on display at a church nearby my home. Now readers of this book are reporting that their prayers are being answered (see pages 35 & 36).

The floral industry (florist, nurseries, associations, societies and others involved with roses) told me "fresh-cut long stem roses have not lived as long as yours!" According to my research it is unheard of to have fresh-cut roses stay actively alive for ten (10) weeks, an historical record. Take note that these roses were delivered by a florist to my house, which were fresh-cut roses, not roses growing outside in my back yard.

"What did you say - ten days or was that ten weeks?" many people asked me. My reply was "They stayed alive for ten weeks." The next response they gave me was, "Fresh cut long stem roses normally stay about one to two weeks, perhaps a little longer. I have never heard of roses lasting as long as yours."

It is indeed appropriate that God made those roses the vehicle for this miracle since roses have been admired throughout history. If you ask ten people to name their favorite flower, probably the majority would name the rose.

These unusual roses came to me on Sweetest Day. It is a holiday held on the third Saturday in October. A man in Ohio started it when he passed small gifts to the under privileged. Later on, others got the idea or remembering everyone with good cheer. It spread to Detroit and other American cities and now is known as "Sweetest Day."

The front page of the Michigan newspaper, *The Eccentric*, Birmingham-Bloomfield Edition, Thursday, Dec. 16, 1999, reported, "Sweetest Day roses still in bloom- 9 weeks later." See this newspaper report on the next page.

Newspaper Report - Front Page

The Eccentric ®

BIRMINGHAM, MICHIGAN • 86 PAGES • http://observer-eccentric.com

Sweetest Day roses still in bloom– 9 weeks later

BY LARRY PALADINO
STAFF WRITER
lpaladino@oe.homecomm.net

It has been nearly nine weeks since a friend sent Lynda Peringian of Bloomfield Township a dozen roses for Sweetest Day.

They're still in full bloom.

"It's a miracle," Peringian said. "It's my second miracle. I wrote a book and that was my first miracle."

Sweetest Day, that made-for-merchants event that is a cash cow for florists and candy makers, was Oct.

> ■ 'It's a miracle.'
>
> *Lynda Peringian*
> *— owner of roses*

16. Roses typically last a week to 10 days. But two weeks later, Peringian's Canadian sweetheart roses, arranged with baby's breath and some ferns, were still looking good.

Halloween came and went. So did

Veterans Day, Nov. 11; Thanksgiving, Nov. 25; Hanukkah, Dec. 4; and even National Pastry Day, Dec. 9.

But day after day, week after week, Peringian's roses still were alive and well.

"We don't really know why," she said.

So she called Affordable Flowers in Birmingham, which had delivered the flowers.

She didn't reach owner John Curzyldo, but she spoke with the

SWEET SMELL: Lynda Peringian with her roses that are still in full bloom nine weeks after Sweetest Day.

Please see ROSE, A8

Rose from page A1

manager Hilda Stewart, who sent out designer Kari Bohl to check out the long-lasting blooms, which were sent with one small package of a powdery substance, Floralife, to dissolve in the vase and make the flowers last.

"Usually we tell customers if they get a week to 10 days out of them they're doing well," Bohl said. "But two months is just unheard of."

She thinks that because

Peringian has the flowers in a breezeway that is very cool, it has helped extend their life.

"Our coolers are 40 degrees," she said.

Peringian even knocked the roses off the table and put them back without a problem, Bohl said.

"They're fully opened, still alive and drawing water," she said.

Those particular flowers, Bohl said, came from Rosalea, a

grower in Canada. The type of rose has a long stem and small head and often is referred to as a tea rose, she said.

Peringian, who said she is a registered dietitian, owns Peringian & Associates, a health care business in Birmingham. She said her book, "Physical and Occupational Health Care Job Search Handbook," was published in 1989 and is used as a textbook by colleges and universities across the country.

9

LIFE OF THE LONG LASTING ROSES

Even though the front page of the newspaper briefly tells you the rose story, many readers have been fascinated about these roses, asking me for more information. Therefore, this book gives all the details and tells the complete story.

We begin with the delivery day, Saturday, Sweetest Day, October 16, 1999, and continue to their end, December 23, 1999. They had an unbelievable long life with no explainable reason causing them to draw water for ten weeks.

The following is the sequence of events::
1. THE DELIVERY DAY
2. FROM TWELVE TO FOUR ROSES
3. MY DREAM
4. DISCOVERY OF ROSES
5. ROSES GET EXAMINED
6. NEWSPAPER REPORT, CALLERS, and VISITORS
7. ROSES LAST DAY
8. PRESERVING the ROSES
9. YEARS LATER (2000 – 2004)
10. HISTORICAL RECORD and *The "MIRACLE ROSES"*

THE DELIVERY DAY

That Saturday in mid-October of 1999 marked a turning point in my life. It was a day just right for an outside cleanup of the colorful maple leaves that covered our lawn. I was outside raking them into piles at the side of the house when a young man in a florist delivery van pulled up and stopped me. He asked me if he had the correct address and said my name.

I told him "Yes, I'm Lynda." He then handed me a bouquet of a dozen roses, and I thanked him. He drove away, and I looked at the pretty roses. They were wrapped in clear plastic wrap, tied with a red ribbon, and smelled very sweet. I glanced at the small card attached and saw that they were from a friend. I noticed there was some baby's breath in with the flowers, along with a few green ferns. They did not come with any water; no vase filled with water, or any small green plastic water tubes.

I often receive fresh cut flowers from friends and family which are either mixed bouquets, carnations, or roses. Sometimes clients also send bouquets to my office, so I did not think much more about this Sweetest Day gift.

My mind returned to the yard work yet to be done, and I placed the rose bouquet on the ground near a leaf pile. They sat there for about fifteen minutes until my mother came out of the house. She walked down the driveway towards me asking me if I was planning on coming in the house to eat lunch. We talked for a while about my progress with the raking, and then she saw the roses.

She took the roses inside the house and removed the plastic wrap, placing them in the plastic pitcher I often used for flowers. She did not cut the stems down. Normally we do not cut the stems when we first get flowers. They are prettier staying long, and I think they live longer. Then, days or a week later, we usually cut the stems and rearrange the bouquet.

My mother then placed tap water in the pitcher, which was city water, not well water. The small package of powdery substance which had come along with the bouquet was opened and was dissolved in the water. Outside the pitcher, she wrapped the red ribbon and tied it with a bow.

FROM TWELVE TO FOUR ROSES

My twelve roses sat for weeks, going back and forth from the kitchen, dining room, and breezeway. They were used as a centerpiece for a luncheon, and many were given away. Visitors admired them, and I gave them some. We took a couple of roses to a friend in the hospital . . . I always like sharing my flowers so other people can enjoy them.

About five weeks after the delivery, one day while rearranging furniture, the roses were knocked off the table. They fell to the floor, and we cleaned up the mess. We cut the stems down on the four remaining roses and put the bouquet in a small glass vase of water.

MY DREAM

Two months after Sweetest Day, on the evening of December 15, I remember saying a short prayer at bedtime, and that night I had a spiritual dream, which was the Lord within me. After waking up the next morning, I thought about this unusual dream. How interesting I thought, that so often we think of our Lord away from us, a distance from us. However, He is within us, as He was in my dream. Why, I wondered, did I have this unusual dream? I had concluded that it was a message to me that a surprise was about to happen. I told myself, "I should be alert to this and keep my eyes open." Many of my dreams before have given me messages and have helped me with decisions to be made and warnings. This has been a positive benefit, and these dreams are an interesting blessing.

DISCOVERY OF ROSES

Placing my spiritual dream in the back of my mind, and being a little more alert than usual, I continued on with my normal activities. I got out of bed in the morning and then helped my dad, who has Alzheimer's disease, get dressed. We had our breakfast, and I started to get our home ready for the holidays.

It was then that I glanced at the vase of roses, noticing that they were still beautiful and alive. "Goodness' sake," I said to myself, " I had actually forgotten all about these roses. I need to add water to them."

I remembered they were delivered to me mid-October, two months earlier. How could this be? It seemed to me my other roses never stayed alive this long. They would last maybe a week or two at best. They received no special attention. Then, I recalled my dream from last night and I told myself, "These roses were the surprise my dream was about." Suddenly, I felt a burst of happiness with my discovery of the roses.

This spiked my curiosity. What variety of roses were they? Luckily, I recalled the delivery man came from a florist a few miles from my home. I phoned the florist and spoke to the manager. After identifying myself and the date of the delivery, she confirmed that the roses were delivered to me for Sweetest Day from my friend Lance.

She was amazed that the roses were still in bloom and asked if she could send someone over to see them. I told her that we would be home and that it was fine to send the lady over. She said that it was unusual for fresh cut long stem roses to live so long.

ROSES GET EXAMINED

After the phone call, the designer arrived at our house. She examined the roses, the baby's breath, and the fern, and said the roses were still alive drawing water. We were asked if they got any special treatment.

"No, they simply came in a plastic wrap, no plastic tubes, and there was no vase filled with water. It is a miracle," I told her. "Probably there would have been more roses remaining, but I gave them away." I also said. Four roses were remaining, and the baby's breath and fern were still in good condition. The designer identified the roses as coming from a grower in Canada.

NEWSPAPER REPORT, CALLERS, and VISITORS

Soon the local newspaper heard about my roses. They sent a photographer to our home, and I was interviewed by a reporter. Their article about the roses hit the front page on Thursday, December 16, 1999. After that, we had people calling, coming to the house to admire the roses, and asking questions. They were asking all kinds of questions, including "What did you do to the roses to make them live so long?"

I replied, "Nothing. We did not do anything special to them. It was God who did it. It was a miracle, and the Bible mentions miracles." Some people agreed, and to others I was refreshing their memory about miracles.

So many people kept calling that I took my phone off the hook. It was getting hard to find a moment to rest from all the excitement. I was getting tired. The local newspaper's front page story was enough; we did not need any more newspaper reports or strangers coming to the house to see the roses. The holidays are what we needed to focus on, not the roses.

ROSES LAST DAY

Providing strength in turbulent times to live each day as it comes, my roses continued to live one more week after they made the newspaper headlines in December. Then we noticed they started to slowly die away . . . one by one.

As I looked at the four roses, I thought about all the attention these unusual roses had attracted with the newspaper report and the visitors who came to see them. How interesting, I had thought that these roses were so unusual to live so long, and there was nothing we did to cause their longevity.

I could tell looking at the roses that they were drying up. They were bending over and getting limp, the color fading, and the leaves were curling. The baby's breath was crumbling and the fern was drying up. Even the sweet smell had diminished. There was nothing I could do . . . their end was fast approaching.

On December 23, 1999, the roses were no longer drinking water; the water had stayed untouched. They ended their life ten weeks after the delivery date of October 16, 1999. Despite the inevitability of death, it seemed to me that these roses had a spirit that was still living.

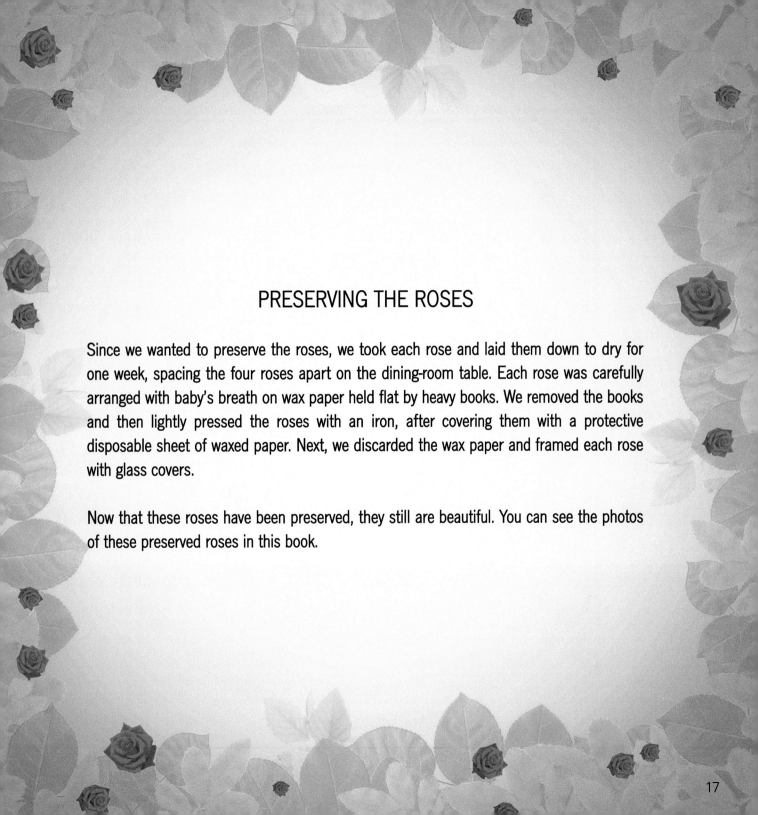

PRESERVING THE ROSES

Since we wanted to preserve the roses, we took each rose and laid them down to dry for one week, spacing the four roses apart on the dining-room table. Each rose was carefully arranged with baby's breath on wax paper held flat by heavy books. We removed the books and then lightly pressed the roses with an iron, after covering them with a protective disposable sheet of waxed paper. Next, we discarded the wax paper and framed each rose with glass covers.

Now that these roses have been preserved, they still are beautiful. You can see the photos of these preserved roses in this book.

Preserved *"MIRACLE ROSE TWO"*

YEARS LATER (2000 – 2004)

Later on, my scientist friend told me that he was not completely convinced that a miracle had occurred. He suggested that we needed to repeat this "experiment" the following year by using the same kind of roses, doing the same treatment, and doing nothing different. "Use the same plastic pitcher, the same water, and do the same thing as before," he told me.

On Sweetest Day 2000, Lance sent me the same kind of roses. We gave them the same treatment as the previous years' roses, and nothing different. I used the same plastic pitcher, the same water, and did nothing else. These fresh cut long stem roses lived about two weeks.

Each Sweetest Day for the next several years, the same kind of roses were delivered to me, and the same treatment followed. Even though Lance was never asked to send me roses, he kept calling the florists, and the roses kept coming the following years – 2001, 2002, 2003, and 2004. They failed to duplicate the ten-weeks-of-life record set by my 1999 roses. None even came close to ten weeks. These new roses all had died within one to two weeks.

HISTORICAL RECORD and *The "MIRACLE ROSES"*

After five years of trying to duplicate the longevity of my 1999 Sweetest Day roses, I finally decided to stop. It was more convincing that a miracle had occurred since I had repeated the experiment for so many years. My special 1999 year roses had not only set an "historical record" of life – ten weeks, but they were also *The "MIRACLE ROSES."*

How interesting that God had created *The "MIRACLE ROSES"* as an excellent vehicle since roses are honored as a popular flower! Roses have been admired for years and these roses revived a belief in miracles. God wants us to believe in miracles and how better to capture a lot of attention than with roses- the "Queen of Flowers."

"Why did God select me?" I thought to myself. Perhaps He knew that I like to help people and that is why I became a healthcare professional. It seemed like He wanted me to write another book and these amazing roses had a story for me to tell. This time my writing assignment was to motivate people in all walks of life to share and help each other, making this a better world.

The *"MIRACLE ROSES"* - A True Story
by Lynda Peringian

SAINT THERESE – My Heavenly Friend

The true story of my *"MIRACLE ROSES"* staying alive for ten weeks was well documented (pages 7-15), including the 1999 newspaper report (page 8), and witnessed by many people. Many people told me their theory of how the roses were able to last so long. This was due to a divine (heaven) intervention (go between) of the intercession (mediation) of God and St. Therese. God has helpers (known as saints). A saint is a holy person who performs many miracles. St. Therese is known for roses, helping people with miracles, and all religions know her. Her ability to work miracles comes from God. She is well liked. People seek her healing and guidance. If you wish to get your prayer answered, see AUTHOR'S ADVICE (page 5).

After years of contemplation and prayers, I am convinced that this theory is correct. My beloved neighbor, Mary Trambush helped make this possible with her prayers to God. She attended The National Shrine of the Little Flower, Royal Oak, Michigan. This worldwide known Michigan church, located nearby my home town is dedicated to St. Therese. Prior to Mary's death, she requested my assistance when she was given word of her terminal illness. I helped Mary and I know she appreciated my work even after her death in 1999. Mary, now in heaven, wanted me to get rewarded for helping her. I believe she asked God to bless me with a unique miracle- the miraculous roses.

Here is how my intercession from God and St. Therese happened with my roses:
1. Mary Trambush was terminally ill in 1998 and 1999. She asked me to help her, which I did.
2. Mary passed away on August 2, 1999. She went to heaven and continued her prayers to God and St. Therese.
3. Delivery day of the roses was on October 16, 1999 (page 10). St. Therese feast month is October.
4. St. Therese relics were on display November 3, 1999 at The National Shrine of the Little Flower. I drove by that cold day noticing the long lines of seventy five thousand people at the church.
5. The intercession from God and St. Therese occurred with my roses possibly when they were delivered, or during the relics tour. The miraculous roses stayed alive for (10) ten weeks!
6. Newspaper report, December 16, 1999 documented the story of the roses still alive (page 8). Also, the roses were witnessed by many people (page 13, 14). They had alot of attention.
7. Roses ended their life on December 23, 1999, an unbelievable long life - ten weeks (page 15).
8. After the newspaper report came out, people were getting positive effects (page 24).
9. People told me the roses lasted so long due to an intercession from God and St. Therese.

10. This book was first published in 2005. Positive effects were occurring (page 25). Praises kept coming in (pages 35 and 36). Reports are still being reported, perhaps right now...this very minute!

11. After years of contemplation and prayers, 1999 - 2010, I was completely convinced that St. Therese's intercession was in 1999. She wanted me to receive The *"MIRACLE ROSES,"* and she knew I would be kind enough to share with others. God wants us to help and share with other people. He blesses us with our good deeds and this helps make a better world to live in.

12. This book is a "Conduit" - helps people connect to God and St. Therese. Divine intervention is working. We are thankful for the miracles and blessings happening daily to readers of this book.

St. Therese is popular with all religions (Jewish, Moslems, Christians, etc.) and some people seem to think she is associated only with Catholics, which is not true. She is noted as the "greatest saint of modern times" and her roses continue to fall everywhere. She is well liked and people seek her healing and guidance. Some people seem to confuse St. Therese with Mother Teresa; the two are completely different people. St. Therese - my heavenly friend, was born in France and entered the convent early in life. She had a life of simplicity and is known as the "Saint of the Little Ways," meaning she believed in doing little things in life well and making others love God. Also, she is known as the "Little Flower, and she thought of herself as being a small flower in a garden. She had said, "After my death, I will let fall a shower of roses. I want to spend my heaven doing good on earth." Many people pray for her intercession and ask for a rose to appear, a sign that their prayers may be answered. St. Therese had suffered tuberculosis and through sickness and darkness, she died at a young age of 24 in 1897. In her autobiography, *"The Story of a Soul,"* the world came to know her. Due to the inspiration of her life and her powerful presence from heaven, she touched the world quickly. Many lives have been touched by her intercessions. One of the first churches in the world and North America is The National Shrine of the Little Flower. It is dedicated in honor of St. Therese. This beautiful church has tours and visitors enjoy seeing the relics of St. Therese. I donated Preserved *"MIRACLE ROSE #3"* (see photo on next page) to this church. Now with this donation, others can enjoy seeing it. A portion of the sale of this book gets donated to worldwide charity groups. Let us continue on further by reading the next section of this book-"MIRACLES," which God wants us to believe in.

Donated to the National Shrine of the Little Flower.

Preserved *"MIRACLE ROSE THREE"*

THE BIBLE IN REFERENCE TO MIRACLES

Religious experts tell us that miracles happen every day, but we do not pay attention to them because they are not awesome. We tend to overlook a lot, taking so many things for granted. Luckily, I had "my eyes open," seeing my roses, which revived a belief in miracles. Miracles happen every day. God will do what He wants and when He wants, since He is in control. God planned my dream, and He also created my roses to live so long, making them *The "MIRACLE ROSES".*

A " miracle" is an event or effect that has no explanation by any known natural law. There is a direct intervention of divine will, since God the Creator can change natural events. The many miracles described in the Bible range from curing physical illnesses and casting a storm to bringing the dead back to life. Those who saw them were amazed and often called them "wonders." Some Old Testament miracles are:

- Exodus 14
- 2 Kings 2: 4-5
- Daniel 6

Albert Einstein once said, "There are only two ways to live your life. One as though nothing is a miracle. The other is as if everything is." It has been said that miracles are God's way of remaining anonymous. His works are visible, and they are in the hands of everyday people like us, showing us the positive hope we wish to know.

POSITIVE EFFECTS OCCURRING

Reading about *The "MIRACLE ROSES"* keeps us more positive, which the world urgently needs. Also seeing with your own eyes a physical object, the roses, which you can touch, feel, and smell, makes us believe even more that miracles do happen. With the endless litany of earthquakes, fires, terrorist attacks, unemployment, and other bad events besieging us, we need to read about some good news to help us keep more positive.

God gives His people a dream. When God deals with us and wants us to eliminate negativity in a life, He gives us a dream to help us keep more positive. Do you know God's dream for you? How can you make your dream come true? Get in touch with your own feelings. This is where the dream must start. And you have to be enthused about your dream. Then ask yourself, "What do I really want to accomplish?" God will get in touch with your own feelings, and you will get in tune with God's spirit.

God wants us to have faith in Him. He wants us to have hope, think positive, and believe in miracles. *The "MIRACLE ROSES"* has caused profound and positive effects on me and others (family, friends, and readers of the newspaper report).

The following are the POSITIVE EFFECTS OCCURING since 1999:

1. People have gained inspiration, hope, and faith, which keeps getting passed on from one person to another... on and on. People are getting uplifted, which is needed in our world of problems.

2. People learn, and/or their memory gets refreshed, that the Bible mentions miracles.

3. One person, a nonbeliever, becomes more convinced about God and miracles. This person then convinces another, which has a ripple effect.

4. People get motivated to share and help others. God will bless you with your good deeds.

5. This book, The *"MIRACLE ROSES" - A True Story* works as a conduit to God and St. Therese. It helps as a connector to help people.

6. Readers of this book are reporting good news of intercession and inspiration (see pages 35 and 36). These are a sample... more remarkable stories still being collected. They keep coming in from everywhere since the printing of this book... even today.

Peringian says "Try to focus on your prayer while you read this book. Keep it simple, not a large list." Perhaps right now, as you are reading this book, a positive effect has passed on to you. Maybe something good will happen or a rose will appear to you, which has happened to some readers.

KEEP YOUR EYES OPEN

That December morning when I discovered my roses, if you recall earlier, I had told you that I had a spiritual dream the night before. The dream had alerted me that a surprise was to happen. By staying more alert, I kept my eyes more wide open.

My aunt used to tell me to be alert when I was a little girl. Aunt Rose also said "Lynda, keep your eyes open and look around." It was a coincidence that her name was "Rose." This brings up an interesting point. We need to pay attention to what is happening all around us more often. By doing this, we may discover things we take for granted. So often we tend to take so much for granted. God creates miracles all the time. Every day there are miracles occurring.

Surprisingly, some readers of this book have reported roses appearing to them. These reports of the roses have been red or white in color, and usually fresh cut or silk. It is a mystery to me if other colors will be reported.
St. Therese did say, *"After my death, I will let fall a shower of roses."*
Here are a couple of the "PRAISES" referring to roses (pages 35 and 36):
> Connie Simmons - Davidson, MI said *"a live red rose in the middle of the road!"*
> Judi Pelli - Michigan reported *"a single red rose on the floor!"*

Keep your eyes open and look around. Who knows what you will find? Maybe it will be something good, and/or another miracle, such as I did when I discovered those amazing roses.

PRAYERS

Prayers are important in keeping yourself positive and in maintaining inner peace. By thinking deeply, continuously in mental reflection, you are dwelling on a subject in your mind. By repeating over and over your thoughts in prayer, God will hear you and He listens to what you say. Keep your dream alive.

Read your Bible and your prayer book. Pray about your thoughts and have patience. Someone once said, "inch by inch, life is a cinch, but yard by yard, life is hard."

Take time for saying your prayers in your daily life even if it is just a few minutes. Perhaps you know someone now who is ill and needs more faith and hope in their life. Maybe you are in pain now and need to get help. Prayers are needed for:

- all nations worldwide for peace,
- our President and all in civil authority,
- clergy and people
- all conditions of men, women, and children everywhere.

When we pray, we need to not only ask for what we are desiring, but we need to also thank God for our many blessings, which we do have. Each moment is all we need and not more. All we have is today, and who knows what tomorrow will bring? Be happy for the moment and enjoy it. Let your happiness show through your actions that you love others, even if it is a simple smile. If we all do this, this world would be a better place.

This is one of my favorite sayings: *Yesterday was history*
Today is a gift
Tomorrow is a mystery

St. Therese is known for a prayer called *"MY NOVENA ROSE PRAYER."*
Here is a verse of this prayer: *St. Therese, help me to always*
Believe as you did, in God's great
Love for me, so that I might
Imitate your "Little Way" each day.

When people seem overwhelmed in dealing with daily problems, I share with them the often-heard wisdom of just taking one day at a time. A favorite prayer of mine is "One Day at a Time," by Annie Johnson Flint.

ONE DAY AT A TIME

ONE DAY at a time, with its failures and fears,
With its hurts and mistakes, with its weakness and tears,
With its portion of pain and its burden of care,
One day at a time we must meet and must bear.

One day at a time to be patient and strong;
To be calm under trial and sweet under wrong;
Then its toiling pass and its sorrow shall cease;
It shall darken and die, and the night shall bring peace.

Not yesterday's load we are called on to bear;
Nor the morrow's uncertain and shadowy care;
Why should we look forward or back with dismay?
Our need, as our mercies, are but for one day.

One day at a time, and the day is His day;
He hath numbered its hours, though they haste or delay.
His grace is sufficient; we walk not alone;
As the day, so the strength that He giveth His own.

Annie Johnson Flint

Preserved *"MIRACLE ROSE FOUR"*

ROSE RELAXATION EXERCISE

Relaxation lowers stress and anxiety, increases your strength and stamina, and allows you to enjoy life more. Each person progresses at his or her own rate, and we should take time in our busy schedules to relax.

We just read about prayers and now this next section, relaxation, also can be helpful in keeping positive. Relaxation lowers stress and anxiety, increases your strength and rate, and my advice is take time in your busy schedules to relax. Here is a way you can achieve relaxation, "Rose Relaxation Exercise," and the steps are:

1. Pick a location in your home which is quiet and free of distractions.
2. Take a rose and place it in front of you. You can take any type of rose - a fresh cut rose, a silk rose, or a dried rose.
3. Sit back and relax in a comfortable position . . . whether it be on a chair, a couch, or the floor. There is no hurry, so take your time.
4. Look at the rose, seeing all its beauty . . . and notice all the petals, the way they fold, and the pretty color. See the green leaves and the long stem.
5. Try not to let other thoughts take you away. Try to focus on what is on your mind.
6. Concentrate on your prayer and ask God for whatever you are trying to achieve.
It is important that we also take time to thank our Lord for our many blessings.
7. Think of the rose and the garden it came from, the sunlight which came upon it. Smell the rose, if it is alive, and take time to enjoy its fragrance.

Hopefully you will feel a healing power enter your soul, and you will have a sense of achievement, peace, hope, and encouragement. Please note that this exercise is not meant to be a substitute for your place of worship. It is simply a suggestion for you to try at home. Use it when you feel the need to relax, get regrouped, or pray.

INFORMATION ABOUT ROSES

Tracing back thousands of years, roses were grown by ancient civilizations. Roses figured prominently in Chinese, Egyptian, Greek, and Roman cultures. Roses were the embodiment of love, spirituality, and beauty in the Middle Ages. Progressing through history, the cult of the rose becomes more general, from the beginning of the European gardens and advancing to become a decorative symbol of earthly love.

Poets, painters, artists, and writers for centuries have captured their beauty in words and pictures. From ancient time to today, people have honored roses as the "Queen of Flowers." Roses also have a history as medicinal and perfume plants. They make an immediate impression with their soft, gentle petals and vivid intense color. When you smell a rose, its fragrance is exquisite . . . a priceless scent that contributes greatly to its popularity. The "Rose of Sharon," mentioned in the Bible, has a large hibiscus shrub with lovely flowers (several colors - rose, purple, white, and blue).

This beloved flower was selected by the United States Congress as this country's national flower. In addition to having been linked to world peace, roses are connected to the three spheres of life: love, death, and Elysium (place of ideal happiness). Roses further permeate American tradition on New Year's Day, with the annual Rose Parade and Rose Bowl football game, held in Pasadena, California. This festival features floral floats and is viewed by millions of people worldwide.

Among the many varieties of roses are those like mine, referred to as "tea roses." The first tea roses came from China on ships carrying tea, owned by the East India Trading Company. The long trip may have made the roses smell like tea, which may be the origin of their name. However, these roses do not smell like tea by themselves. Although tea roses come in many colors, mine were red with a little orange tint, making them attractive in the bouquet with baby's breath and green fern.

CONCLUSION

Thanks to our Lord for all the unimaginable discoveries in our world. Often being occupied in our relentless pursuit of searching for gold, money, or other earthly material, we fail to pay attention to what is around us. It is mind-boggling what we can find. When the author discovered those amazing roses, not only was this an historical record of roses, but these miraculous roses are GOOD NEWS for everyone!

Readers of this book are reporting good news of intercessions and inspiration. Report are constantly coming in. One of the reports, Joan Cox, Sarasota, Florida said, *"Not only was this book extremely helpful to lift your spirit, but everyone will benefit in our tough economic times now."* Our world is suffering not only from the economy, earthquakes, and fires, but so many other problems. This book, which is the story of *The "MIRACLE ROSES"* serves as an excellent tool to lift our spirit, which is badly needed.

The Bible does say "Nothing is ever impossible with God." Believe in miracles and remind others that miracles happen every day. Whether or not your prayer gets answered, either way, say "Thank you God. I have many blessings and appreciate them all." Do not take things for granted. GOD IS IN CONTROL all the time!

AUTHOR'S ADVICE - Four (4) Steps
How You Can Get Your Prayer Answered- Spiritual Connection

This book is a "Conduit"- helps people connect to God and St. Therese. God has helpers, known as saints. *("Here is the patience of the saints; ...* Revelation 14-12). St. Therese is known for roses & working miracles. She had a life of being simple. People seek her healing & guidance and she is known as the "greatest saint" of all times. All religions known her (Jewish, Moslems, Christians, etc). She said, *"I will spend my heaven in doing good on earth and I will let fall a shower of roses."* She died in 1897, and has kept her promise. Miracles and so many good things are happening everyday to people all over the world. See PRAISES (pages 6 & 7).

If you wish to get your prayer answered, the following is my advice as you read this book. AUTHOR'S ADVICE (as you read this book and pray to God). Do these four (4) steps:
1. Pray to God (who gets our glory), one prayer request only (not more than one). Keep it simple.
2. Have faith - be a believer of God (the Creator) & miracles. (Nothing is ever impossible with God).
3. Keep focusing on your prayer while praying to God. St. Therese helps connect to God.
4. Say this, *"Thank you God. Whether or not my prayer gets answered, I have many blessings and appreciate them all."*

Some people report that within a few days, they receive their prayer request. Many others tell me they read this book on another day and continue to focus on their prayer. Then, it happens that their wish is answered! Prayer requests for others are often asked upon and received. If you do not believe in all of my four steps, it may not work. As you continue reading, focus on your prayer. Find a quiet place without distractions and stay positive. Some readers report after they receive a prayer request, they find a rose. If a rose appears to your unexpectingly, perhaps St. Therese sent it. She often leaves a rose as a sign of her presence and calling card. You are surprised. It is a nice blessing from God & St. Therese!

Lynda Peringian

Preserved *"MIRACLE ROSE ONE"*

Printed in the United States
by Baker & Taylor Publisher Services